The
Fall
of Ireland

A novella

Dermot Bolger

NEW ISLAND

PRINT ISBN: 978-1-84840-187-7
EPUB ISBN: 978-1-84840-188-4
MOBI ISBN: 978-1-84840-189-1

British Library Cataloguing Data. A CIP catalogue record for
this book is available from the British Library

Typeset by JM InfoTech INDIA
Cover design by Nina Lyons
Printed by TJ International Ltd, Padstow, Cornwall

New Island received financial assistance from
The Arts Council (An Comhairle Ealaíon), Dublin, Ireland

10 9 8 7 6 5 4 3 2 1

By the same author

Walking the Road*
The Parting Glass*
Tea Chests & Dreams

Poetry
The Habit of Flesh
Finglas Lilies
No Waiting America
Internal Exiles
Leinster Street Ghosts
Taking My Letters back
The Chosen Moment
External Affairs*
The Venice Suite*

Editor
The Picador Book of Contemporary Irish Fiction (UK)
The Vintage Book of Contemporary Irish Fiction (USA)

*(*Available from New Island)*

The Minster had travelled on to Tianjin and Shangri. The other officials had travelled there too, leaving Martin alone here, being chauffeured in silence through the streets of Beijing. His assigned translator sat silently beside him in the back of the limousine. This Chinese interpreter, who had worked diligently at Martin's side all day, was not just skilled in several languages but attuned to recognising those moments when nothing further was required to be said. Perhaps he thought that Martin's silence stemmed from upset at not having been asked to travel on with the remainder of the official Irish delegation, but in truth Martin was merely exhausted. He was talked out and smiled out and bowed out for Ireland: he had given so much of himself to everyone he met during the succession of pointless meetings all day that now he simply felt hollowed out to his core. He had simply nothing more to give to anyone today.

Martin had no problem with being left behind in Beijing. He knew there was no logistical need for him to accompany the Minister to the additional meetings in those other cities. In fact, there was no real need for Martin to be among the team of Irish senior civil servants who accompanied him to Beijing. His Minister was not even a proper government Minister: he merely possessed the illusionary status of all Junior Ministers – or Ministers of State, as their increasingly bloated ranks were subtly rebranded. Junior Ministers were essentially eunuchs, granted the public bauble of a state car and driver to compensate for not being allowed to actually sit or speak at the Cabinet table, where real power resided and real decisions were made.

Not that real decision making would even take place at the Cabinet table for much longer: this government was shuffling to its end. Experienced senior official servants like Martin could sense its death throes being played out. It stood no earthly chance of being re-elected. The unlikely shotgun marriage between the Greens and Fianna Fail was over, except for some final bickering conducted by the junior partner from behind the safety of their babies and their tweets. This cowardly behaviour disgusted the ageing Fianna Fail warhorses, who, for now, were strapping themselves to rocks like so many dying Cuchulains, holding their enemies at bay with the threat that they might raise their heavy swords one final time, before they toppled forward into oblivion and were lost amid the vast depths of their pension pots.

The old regime was still clinging on, but by now it was a smoke-and-mirrors illusion. The International Monetary Fund was already ensconced in Dublin, crunching numbers in hotel suites, discreetly conferring with the European Central Bank while treating Ireland's floundering government with the exaggerated courtesy that is invariably shown to the terminally ill. This was a fallen government in everything but name. All that remained for it were St Patrick's Day trips like this: attempts to preserve the niceties of diplomatic protocol and convey the impression that life was continuing as normal, in much the same way as quarrelling parents try to convey that impression for the sake of the children.

Was Martin's marriage also finished in all but name? Some nights, lying awake in the spare bed in the converted attic, the evidence convinced him that it was. But just now, being silently driven through this congested Beijing traffic, it seemed impossible to imagine any future in which Rachel and he would not be together – bickering or barely speaking until they patched up their latest quarrel – but so indelibly bound by the invisible threads of thirty years of shared love that Martin could conceive of no world without her at the centre of his existence.

Perhaps this was his greatest failing: a failure of imagination. Illusion – not imagination – was his forte. The Minister was in China to maintain the illusion that Ireland had not already ceded its economic independence. Martin was in China to prop up the illusion that his Minister was a politician of substance.

At the time of the Minister's appointment, this three-card trick had been regarded as vital to the next election. This was why state cars were given to minor politicians in remote swing constituencies: so they could be publicly seen, parked outside meetings in parish halls or nosing their way into prominent positions in funeral processions that traversed byroads awash with potholes and floating voters. State cars, and their attendant police drivers, were the manifest illusion of national power. They represented the majesty of government brought home to small villages by local men and women made good, figures who smoothly pretended to represent the allure of real power.

Having a Junior Minister was not as prestigious for a parish as possessing an All Ireland winning hurling medallist, in whose reflective glory everyone could bask. But no All Ireland medallist could speed through a passport in a hurry or smooth over the inconvenience of needing to retrospectively apply for planning permission. Political power was about presenting the illusion that you could magically make problems disappear. To be perceived as being powerful, you needed to be surrounded by people seen as subservient to you: you needed special advisors, minions, folder-holders and door-openers to flesh out the backdrop of your every trick, in the same way as even the best magician needed the distraction of a long-legged assistant in a revealing skirt and shimmering tights.

But when not basking in the local glow of their constituencies, Junior Ministers were essentially the pack mules of government, dispatched to fulfil second-string vaudeville engagements. Sometimes they executed these mundane meet-and-greet tasks with an incandescent arrogance, born from the frustration at being so close, and yet utterly removed, from the actuality of power. But Martin's present Minister – the first rule any civil servant learnt when dealing with a Junior

Minister was to ban the word 'junior' from all conversations – bore his Sherpa-like duties with good grace.

An ageing, silver-haired career politician, he had languished for a decade in the limbo of the Seanad – where brilliant voices so brilliantly convinced themselves of their own brilliance that, at times, it seemed barely important that this second, upper chamber possessed no function beyond serving as a waiting-room and a recovery ward. In the last election Martin's Minister had finally delivered a Dáil seat in the most unpromising of marginal rural constituencies in Munster. In a master-class in vote gathering, he scraped together the vital seventh- and eighth-preference votes that allowed him to fill the fifth seat, by a process of elimination, without reaching the quota.

He had been rewarded by being made a Minister of State, because in the government's euphoric early days there was even talk that – provided his profile was correctly manipulated – he might bring home a running mate with him at the next election. This plan had required him to continue the forensic constituency work for which he was renowned while nationally the party hoped to cultivate the deception that he was a figure of substance. However, any hopes of returning a running mate had disappeared because of the economic devastation his government wrought across Ireland. The nation was essentially bankrupt. Indeed Martin suspected that – rather than face annihilation at the polls – his Minister would retire, along with most of his ageing colleagues, when the forthcoming election was called. For now, however, they needed to maintain the impression that the regime had not fallen.

It was more than just Ministers who planned to jump ship. The two most senior officials accompanying the Minister to China had each told Martin of their plans to take early retirement, before the incoming government were ordered by their foreign paymasters to slash public service pension entitlements. They were urging Martin to do likewise while he still could, telling him that he risked losing a fortune if he actually remained at his post. Factually these men were right, but they were also happily married.

Last year Rachel had taken early retirement from her post of assistant principal in a private feeder primary school in Goatstown, after an INTO advisor explained the financial advantages of doing so. It had left her with a satisfactory pension and the dissatisfaction of a sudden void in her life. So many of their generation were deserting the public service that it felt like the Fall of Saigon. But the men within his department joining the scramble for the last helicopters were all were low-handicap golfers, unlike Martin, who detested the game. When God was inventing the Seanad for washed-out politicians whose careers were essentially over, he had also created the Island Golf Club and Royal Dublin for retired civil servants. But fifty-five was too young for Martin to buy a caddy car and enter God's Waiting Room. It was undeniable that the projected figures in an envelope in his suit pocket proved he would save money in the long term by retiring early. The question was, would being at home seven days a week with a wife already lured into premature retirement save or destroy what remained of his marriage?

It was hard to believe he had spent thirty-seven years in government departments, whose convoluted titles changed almost as frequently as the Ministers who ran them. It had made him adept at distinguishing between illusion and reality. Illusions could often seem more realistic, because more effort needed to be made to painstakingly prop them up. In recent years this was the sensation he sometimes experienced in his marriage:

the sense that Rachel was carefully conjuring an illusion when her friends from bridge or her pottery class called in. Nobody else might notice it, but he could see her automatically start to act out a part: so animatedly manifesting the love which Martin had once taken for granted that he was unsure who she was most trying to convince – their visitors or herself?

It perturbed him because Rachel had never been an actress before: what he had immediately loved was her inability to be anything other than utterly true to herself. But since her retirement there was a part of her that he no longer knew. Was she missing him during these few days apart or was she relieved at not having to maintain the illusion of harmony? Only when he went away on trips like this did she seem able to directly express her love like before. Her endearments in texts and emails seemed tender and genuine, in keeping with the old Rachel. It was as if she could only reconnect to the tapestry of their shared lives together – the almost claustrophobic closeness they once enjoyed – when Martin was physically absent, dispatched abroad to discreetly massage the ego of a Junior Minister.

Not that his present charge needed much ego stroking, merely an assurance that glowing updates about every meeting he attended in China were being emailed, firstly to the editors of the three local papers in his Munster constituency, and then to the Department of the Taoiseach. Martin preferred to work for such ageing apparatchiks, primarily appointed for geographical reasons. They were easier to manage than tiresomely ambitious young Junior Ministers always desperate to make an impression. Not that Martin hadn't evolved stratagems for dealing with the hotshot young Turks that any shrewd Taoiseach learnt to keep close, knowing it was better to have ambitious wannabes pissing out of the Cabinet tent rather than pissing in, and how their undisguised lust for promotion was a useful tool to keep older Ministers in line.

During his early years in the service he occasionally had hard cases to contend with. Martin still remembered a communiqué reaching his desk in 1982 from a newly appointed Junior Minister for Fisheries and Forestry, the late Sean McEllistrim – a barely legible scrawl on the back of a cigarette packet, which a minion had carefully stapled onto official notepaper: '*Give Michael Joe Brady from Dingle the grant for a boat.*' Back then McEllistrim was an unwavering Haughey loyalist, when Charles Haughey needed backwoods simpletons who would die for him. For all the jokes within the department about McEllistrim being barely able to read or write, he had possessed the shrewd cunning of a street fighter who knows that the only true politics is local and every vote counts – be it a first or fifth preference on a ballot paper. Sometimes when trading anecdotes with other officials over dinner, Martin would ponder whether it was his decision to discreetly misfile this scrawled instruction on a cigarette packet that caused McEllistrim to lose his seat to Dick Spring in the next election – by only four votes on the twelfth count.

But now, as the black embassy limo pulled up outside his five-star hotel in Beijing, Martin knew that this was wishful thinking. The truth was that during all his years of diligent work Martin had never exercised true influence on any real decision. He was respected for being good at his job. His job was to take notes, to remember small details diligently and occasionally forget them, to manifest his presence at the beginning and end of meetings and to render himself invisible during any important discussions that took place in between. It helped that he had gradually trained himself to inhabit the sort of personality that could refrain from personality. Strangers genuinely enjoyed meeting him and rarely remembered him afterwards. He was not one of those fire-fighting civil servants who specialised in crisis-management, although – if called upon – Martin's advice could be sharp and brutal. His speciality lay in babysitting Junior Ministers: dealing with their chomping ambition, their thwarted hopes, their frustration at perpetually being one step away from taking on the role of grown-up decision-makers.

To be a Minister of State was to exist in a permanent state of arrested adolescence. This experience should have made Martin adept at dealing with his three adolescent daughters, whose desperate yearning to achieve adult status kept constantly conflicting with their yearning to cling to the protective trappings of childhood. They lived in a world of patched-up teddy bears and childish cotton pyjamas, with demands for super tuck-ins into bed at night: a world of suspended innocence punctuated by furious rows over fake tan and skirts so short as to make a Mongolian prostitute blush, when they set out amid packs of similarly semi-naked classmates, to attend the Wes disco in Donnybrook every Saturday.

Martin had spent so many Saturday nights parked outside this rugby club disco, waiting to collect his girls, that at times he felt like a kerb-crawler there, eyes perpetually drawn to the forbidden teenage flesh being flaunted past him – schoolgirls from Alex and the Institute and Mount Anville and Pembroke and Loreto Foxrock, pimped up as if setting forth to attend a fancy dress party populated by all tarts and no vicars. The twins, Aisling and Aoife, and their younger sister by a year, Clio, (at thirteen, Cliona had declared that her real name was now Clio) loved him deeply. They needed him as a reassuring presence to be there for them. He recognised that at other times they needed him not to be there. But did Rachel still need him to be there for her? If so, then surely, even just once during the past two years, she would have slept with him?

The embassy driver was holding open the limousine door now in the hotel forecourt. Three doormen hovered, anxious to play their part in the pantomime of whisking him inside into the vast lobby. Two impossibly thin and beautiful young Chinese women waited just inside the glass doors, employed for no other reason than to smile in welcome and reassure him of his importance during the few steps that it took to reach the concierge's desk, where a team of porters beamed at him. Then it was the turn of the half dozen receptionists, who worked at the vast reception desk, to look up and smile as he walked past them and entered the lift. He felt foolish because he had misplaced his room key and the lift doors refused to close until he inserted it in a special slot.

Eventually he found it in his pocket and could press the button for his floor. To his relief the doors closed. He wondered if all those Chinese faces paid to watch him make his way across the lobby would now cease to smile. What were their actual lives and working conditions like? What were they like as individuals? Martin would never know. They would always remain an orchestra of carefully choreographed smiles, and he would be just another foreign VIP to them: a figure from a distant world disappearing into a gilded lift, where the security card system – designed to prevent pimps from prowling the corridors at night – provided one further barrier between the hotel's closeted guests and any sense of the real China outside.

Martin felt like a fraud at such moments, when people were employed to create the illusion of importance as he walked through a public space, as if the mere fact of being surrounded by minor functionaries was evidence of being a figure of substance. In reality Martin was a relatively minor civil servant: reliable, pleasant, good with people and good with figures. But his only function here in China was to do exactly what those impossibly thin girls with perfect smiles were doing as they hovered near the glass doors of the hotel lobby: to dress the backdrop to the scene and make somebody else look important by his diffident submissiveness.

Tonight, his diffident presence wasn't even needed. The Minster had travelled on to Tianjin and Shangri with just three advisors – two of them experts in job creation and international co-operation who could be relied upon to do the real work, and the third advisor (the Minister's second cousin), whose sole function was to keep him briefed on any possible electoral fallout from the recent flash-flooding in his constituency. China was important to Ireland – one of the few economies with the cash to buy the bonds that might allow Ireland to keep its sovereignty. However, in terms of local photo ops for pictures to be sent back to regional editors, Martin noted that it was not considered sufficiently important for a full Cabinet Minister to be assigned to do the ritual St Patrick's Day round of meetings here.

The Taoiseach was – as ever – in Washington, presenting the US President with a crystal bowl of shamrock, which officials from the US Department of Agriculture would immediately incinerate. The Minister for Finance was in Germany for public smiles and private crisis-talks. Other Ministers had chosen Australia and New Zealand and San Francisco, knowing that their reign was nearing its end and this was their last chance to immerse themselves in the trappings of protocol. Nobody of importance within the Cabinet had wanted this China gig. There had been no big parade here, merely a minuscule and carefully policed procession of a few dozen people amid freezing snow in a local park. This minuscule parade had still made the main news on Chinese television, because parades were so rarely allowed in Beijing. No real Minister had wanted to walk the diplomatic tightrope involved in having to carefully avoid any meaningful mention of contentious human rights issues in meetings, while still being required to touch upon the issue in a tangential way, to prevent the junior government partners from choking on their Ryvita and heroically issuing a tweet of protest.

Martin had attended four meetings in Beijing before the Minister left, in addition to a black-tie ball organised by expats in a swanky hotel, where Irish developers and entrepreneurs still partied on St Patrick's night in a way that people no longer partied back at home. The embassy had created a daily itinerary for Martin in his Minister's absence and he was expected back for drinks there this evening. But now, as he entered his bedroom and locked the door so he could finally be alone, he felt drained of energy. He had been smiling all day, jovial with his driver and translator, serious and statesmanlike in the token meetings the embassy had set up with minor Chinese officials without ever briefing him about what these meetings were meant to discuss. But his Chinese counterparts had also known that the meetings were about nothing beyond creating an illusion that two nations were communicating, going through the motions of appearing to have discussed issues amid a shadow-play of handshakes and empty phrases.

None of it had been real. He had not truly connected with another human being all day. He had been himself and yet he had turned himself into whatever vision of a minor diplomat people needed to see. He had put people at their ease by affecting levity or gravitas where appropriate. Now he couldn't do it any more. For these few hours at least he needed to be himself for real – whoever that real person was. The driver was due to call back for him, but nobody would notice if he did not return to the embassy to wander about – smiling and lost – amid cocktail drinking diplomats and expats buoyed by nostalgia and historical grudges. He could not even talk honestly to anyone there about how Ireland was falling apart. The government had a new phrase for such honesty: they termed it 'economic treason'.

There were more meetings scheduled for tomorrow when he would smile and virtually small-talk himself to death for Ireland. But tonight he was going nowhere, or certainly nowhere in a diplomatic limousine. He could go out alone if he asked the concierge to arrange for a taxi to Bar Street – the suitably functional name the Chinese had bestowed on a street crammed with foreign bars. But he didn't want crowds or blaring music or the need to pretend that he was having a good time, alone and adrift in a foreign city. Were there brothels on Bar Street? He didn't know, because there were coded routes into the underworld of any city that you could never ask an embassy driver to crack. Martin had never been inside a brothel and fifty-five did not seem like a good age to start. Though exploring the fringes of those semi-licit worlds had been part of the allure of his early junkets abroad, walking through the red light district of Amsterdam or the Reeperbahn in Hamburg, curious to observe what was on view, but aware that he didn't have it in him to do more than observe, and would sooner die than be unfaithful to Rachel.

Was he too moral for infidelity, or simply too cowardly? Did the answer need to be definitively one or the other? He was just himself, the sum of his contradictions and past mistakes, suddenly homesick in a luxury foreign hotel and desperately scared because of the sense he'd had for some time now that home was slipping away from him. It was a ridiculous thought, but if he simply walked out of this hotel and disappeared, who would miss him in any meaningful sense, beyond the initial shock Rachel and their daughters would feel? If his plane crashed on the way home, there would be platitudes and compensation and genuine tears from his daughters, but the twins and Clio were essentially women, on the cusp of no longer needing him. They would recover from his death, but what would Rachel allow herself to feel? A reawakening of the first love that once made them inseparable? Maybe it was too late to expect that to ever return. Maybe there was just too much resentment harboured over remarks he made when stressed out; too many times when she had felt betrayed because he did not automatically take her side in rows with the girls or with neighbours.

Thirty-seven years in the civil service had trained him to meditate and always try to locate the middle ground, to find a fudged set of compromises that allowed them to live side by side with neighbours they frequently detested on that competitive Killiney estate of pristine lawns and flotillas of hanging flower baskets. Compromises were what you safely lived by, but irrational passion was what you fucked by. Perhaps if Martin had shouted at the solicitor next door for cutting down the overhanging branch from their tree at dawn two years ago without having the courtesy to ask their permission; maybe if he had gone out on one of the nights back then and told the pompous prick to fuck himself and to fuck his stupid barbeques that went on until four a.m. under Rachel's bedroom window, presided over by his dyed-blonde wife who probably possessed a bigger black box than a jumbo jet, maybe then – after Martin had come back in from the garden, having destroyed neighbourly relations for at least a decade – Rachel might have called him into the bedroom they once shared, beside herself with glee, and, having extracted every detail from him, fucked his brains out.

But if Martin had strayed so far out of character to achieve such a pyrrhic victory on that one night, Rachel would have hated going out to her car ever since then in case she met their boorish neighbours after her initial thrill of revenge had subsided. Rachel would never have felt comfortable again sunbathing in the back garden; her life dictated by a careful avoidance of the people next door. Rachel had thought it was cowardice that stopped him going out to confront their neighbour, but it had actually been for her sake, so that her life would not be poisoned by the miasma of angry words left hanging in the air.

Besides, Martin knew that life had its own way of extracting revenge. Those all-night barbeques no longer occurred, with Rachel forced to lie awake and listen to the drone of the solicitor's voice boasting of all the buy-to-let mortgages he was able to juggle like a gigolo juggles rich lovers. The only reason why the banks had not yet foreclosed on him and hundreds of investors like him was to avoid a glut of unsellable property going on the market at once. Their neighbour was a fallen man, entangled in arrears on numerous mortgages on rental properties. Martin's contact in the Department of Justice had quietly tipped Martin off that he was under investigation by the Law Library and the fraud squad for dipping into money from client accounts simply to keep his messy pretence of prosperity going. Martin made a point of waving to him most mornings, enjoying how the man was unaware that Martin knew he was living on borrowed time, with a court case and professional disbarment beckoning. The house next door would soon to put up for sale. The brochure would feature a photo of the back garden, enhanced by Rachel's beautiful adjoining tree, scarred only by a needlessly amputated branch.

Rows with neighbours were one thing, but the increasingly intense rows between Rachel and the girls tore at his very soul. His attempts to broker peace at home seemed to have done the most to drive Rachel away from him. He wanted to take her side and generally did so, but sometimes – if she was exhausted or caught up in some unspoken worry of her own – she could be irrational in her reaction to even simple requests from the girls. On those occasions, it was not that he was siding with the girls against her; he was trying to find some consensus that would not result in screaming matches or one party or the other slamming doors and sulking.

Martin never understood why Rachel could not see this, because these days she frequently expressed a newfound hatred for her father, which seemed to stem from how the man invariably took her late mother's side – regardless of who was right or wrong – during every argument between mother and daughter when Rachel was a rebellious teenager. Her childhood had undoubtedly scarred Rachel, though it seemed as if it were only now, with time weighing on her hands after her premature retirement, that she understood it. Outward appearances and unquestioned parental authority were the twin pillars of the squeezed, middle-class poverty in which she had grown up in Limerick, a poverty that stemmed not so much from an absence of money as from her father's inability to spend it. Limerick city was small enough to be dissected by invisible fault-lines of social caste, with many girls attending Laurel Hill Convent, run by French nuns, under strict instructions never to consort on the street with girls like Rachel from less posh convent schools.

Martin's father-in-law was the sort of harmless, well-intentioned doctor who voted Fine

Gael and loved West End musicals, the late General Franco and right-wing causes. His inability to convey parental affection to his only daughter chimed with his abrupt bedside manner. His tone suggested to patients that, while their condition was not terminal, he would prefer to be paid in cash, just in case. Doctor O'Farrell had sold the family home in Limerick, along with his medical practice, after he was widowed. He moved to a smaller house in Cork and bought into a colleague's practice in Bishopstown. He never consulted his daughter (by then about to qualify as a primary teacher in Carysford College in Blackrock) about these changes, nor had he shown any cognisance that his departure from Limerick would render Rachel emotionally homeless.

But when Martin knew Rachel first, she was still intensely concerned about her widowed father's welfare. When Aisling, Aoife and Clio were young they would make dutiful trips to Cork to visit him, inviting him into their homes every Christmas and Easter or if he was ever ill. In fact Rachel used to phone him every Sunday to fret about his diet and blood pressure. It was during one such call, three years ago, that Dr O'Farrell mentioned how a new colleague in the Bishopstown medical practice – where he was now semi-retired but still pottered about – had introduced him to the internet; to a touch-screen programme that allowed him to explain ailments to patients using three-dimensional displays of body parts.

The man had sounded mesmerised by the internet, so fascinated in fact that just four months later Rachel and Martin received a wedding invitation, with no explanatory note, inviting them – but not the twins or Clio – to his wedding in the Rochestown Park Hotel. The bride, Mei, a Chinese girl working in Bantry, was two years younger than Rachel and looked at least ten years younger than that. This wedding had virtually ended all contact between Rachel and her father. Now, after several glasses of wine, Rachel would obsess about the damage she felt her father had done by always taking her mother's side, by making her feel like a misfit for simply wanting to be an ordinary teenage girl who wore flared jeans and liked to read *Jackie* magazine. Yet sometimes during arguments with Martin she would suddenly declare, 'At least my father always stood up for his wife, unlike you. Our girls have you wrapped around their little fingers. Say what you want about my father, but he's no pushover. He's a real man.'

Martin knew that it was crazy to be wasting his only free evening in China reliving those irrational rows when Rachel would become consumed with a anger that not even she could fathom; a fury fuelled by her sense of growing older with life passing her by; by the fact that her father, whom she had been dreading nursing through old age, was suddenly happily living a second life with a Chinese woman younger and prettier than his daughter. A new mother-in-law, towards whom Martin had experienced an unexpected and deeply guilty erotic charge on the sole occasion they met, at that awkward wedding, populated by chattering young Chinese girls who seemed intent on inducing coronary attacks among the elderly ranks of provincial medical consultants present and causing apoplectic shock among their disapproving wives.

He wanted to forget about these domestic problems for one night, but he couldn't. Rachel and the girls were his entire life. Crossing the vast bedroom, Martin checked his emails on the computer. There was the usual raft of departmental memos on which he was automatically copied in, then chatty messages from each of the three girls, hurriedly written with uncomplicated love. Rachel's email this evening was warm and affectionate, its sentiments sounding like the Rachel of old, as if the woman with whom he had shared the first twenty-three years of marriage was res-urrected by his absence. Maybe this was how they should communicate at home, he thought, sitting at different computers in different rooms.

Martin spent half an hour emailing replies, inserting small jokes into Rachel's email that he hoped would make her smile. He could envisage every detail of the extended back bedroom where she kept her laptop – the dressing-table awash with jewellery boxes and anti-ageing creams; the antique oak writing bureau now kept closed, but which used to always be crammed with realms of pupils' homework needing to be corrected, the full-length bespoke sliding wardrobes fitted by Lafayettes in Dun Laoghaire. His old bedroom felt more real in his imagination than when he was actually present at home, because here he was free to watch her smiling as she read his reply on her laptop without feeling like an intruder who had strayed into territory where he was no longer welcome.

These thoughts were doing Martin no good. He needed to get out of this bedroom. The hotel had a massive swimming pool, a gym and a luxu-rious spa on an upper floor he had not yet visited. The Minister was in Tianjin and, for tonight at least, Martin was basically on a paid holiday. His daughters would have loved this hotel when they were younger. Not the cold, wide Chinese streets outside where everything would feel too strange, but the vast corridors they could enjoy exploring. He missed those early family holidays: the three girls clinging to him in the swimming pool and Rachel laughing at their antics from her sun lounger, all of them at ease together in that five-star hotel on Lake Garda that they had visited for six years in a row.

More recent holidays felt awkward for being the only time when he and Rachel still shared a room. 'It's an awful pity you don't find a good, clean massage parlour – you know the sort – or have an affair,' Rachel had remarked casually last year, unhurriedly fixing her hair in the hotel bedroom in Tunisia before dinner while the twins sent impatient texts from the lobby to see if he could hurry her up. 'It's apparently what everyone does now: arrange affairs on Internet sites.' She had turned to glance at him, her tone as relaxed as if suggesting he enrol in a course in wine appreciation. 'I honestly wouldn't mind if you did, Martin. I'd understand that it would only be about sex, and I've no interest in sex any more. I'm trying not to be selfish. You shouldn't have to go without pleasure. We're grown-ups. I mean, even my father found someone on the internet and he's been wearing the same horn-rimmed glasses for thirty years.'

Rachel had turned back to the mirror then to check her hair before picking up the handbag that matched her shoes and opening the bedroom door. They rowed about her words, going down in the lift to join their three daughters, with Martin claiming that this was a terrible statement and that if either of them had an affair it would ruin any remaining intimacy. Rachel seemed bewildered by his reaction, repeating with a shrug that she was merely trying to show some consideration for his needs.

They never discussed her words again or what they truly signified. It was like a lot of other things that they no longer discussed because Rachel claimed she was no longer able to deal with his intensity, and the fact that he always made everything too complicated when she merely wanted a simple life now. But Martin no longer possessed any idea of what Rachel really wanted. He realised that he no longer possessed a clear idea of who she truly was since her retirement. He just knew that he must have hurt her in some way that could never be taken back. In their early years he had sometimes provoked rows just for the intensity of the sexual pleasure when they made up, clinging to each other, bodies damp with sweat. But there must have been words said in the heat of some argument that she still held against him; words that could never be any form of foreplay, having congealed into an invisible wall of ice between them.

When he had last tried to talk about this – knowing she got annoyed if he probed into the completely separate life she had made for herself, volunteering to sit on a Third World charity fund-raising committee in between endless classes in Meditation, Mindfulness and Positive Living in a new Pilates studio – she merely said she had wasted years worrying over small things when the girls were young. Now she wanted to live in the moment, and it was time he learnt to do likewise. Maybe Rachel was right: maybe the abrupt termination of her career had showed that you only had one life. He was marooned here at the state's expense. He owed it to himself to prove to her that he could live it up, so that he could fill his email tomorrow with amusing incidents.

Perhaps he should phone that concierge to arrange a taxi to Bar Street. It would beat sitting in this room, drinking alone because he could not sleep, yet being afraid to drink too much in case a hangover interfered with the smooth schedule of his meaningless meetings tomorrow. Beijing was the city where everything was for sale; a city with a different morality, born without original sin. He knew what he really desired tonight, though he had no real wish to see his desires realised. But looking back, just now he felt that he had also missed out on so much, simply from hearing other men talk. He had always held back from impropriety through decency, or caution, or a sense of fidelity to a woman who no longer seemed to need him. But even though he ached for a woman's touch, for the almost forgotten feel of skin against his skin, he was too old to start negotiating with pimps or wandering up stairwells in side streets, alert to the possibility of disease or humiliation or being beaten up or simply made to look plain foolish.

These thoughts were doing him no good. He needed to get out of this bedroom, where loneliness made him a lost soul. He needed to be among people, so he would automatically assume some other persona than simply being a forlorn man. Finding the swimming togs in his suitcase, Martin followed the confusing signage until he reached the leisure complex. Just walking through the corridors allowed him to become somebody different: a civil servant masquerading as an anonymous foreign diplomat. More tall, willowy girls stood compliantly at the reception desk here, more attendants were on hand to respectfully hand him towels. He felt better before he even changed out of his clothes. The forty-metre swimming pool was longer and more luxurious than anything he had seen in a European hotel. He swam ten lengths, enjoying the feel of his body stretching out. At seventeen he had been a Leinster schoolboy champion swimmer, not that this achievement received much acknowledgement in Terenure College, where success on the rugby pitch was the only true currency and passport to success. But he used to love those dawn training swims: just he and two other boys – rugby-refuse-niks, as they called themselves – bored by scrum halves and loosehead props, more obsessed with French new-wave cinema and French girls. Even now he enjoyed occasionally competing in swimming galas, enjoying his daughters' enjoyment at seeing him collect the gold medal in his age category.

Simply being here in the water restored to him another layer of identity, a link to a time before

Rachel or the girls when he was simply himself, unhindered by any other thoughts during training except how to make the perfect dive and execute his tumble-turn, conscious of being in his true element in the water and propelled by a fierce determination to beat anyone.

He rested now in the water, aware that his show of stamina had earned the respect of the two Chinese pool attendants. After some moments he commenced another ten fast lengths, not being showy or pushing the pace but remaining utterly in control. One pool attendant handed him a fresh towel when he emerged from the water, and Martin knew from this young man's look that he was also a serious swimmer. There was so much they could talk about, just like there were so many facets of life he could meaningfully discuss with people in this hotel, yet Martin knew that more than a language barrier separated them. He nodded his thanks to the attendant, aware that circumstances made it impossible for them to communicate in any meaningful way.

The steam room and sauna were segregated. A few Chinese businessmen or party officials sat there naked, talking quietly. Occasionally one of them lifted himself clear of the water with a flash of white buttocks and dropped, feet first, into the freezing cold plunge pool. As Martin towelled himself off, he was perturbed by how his eye kept being drawn to this sight. A gay colleague in the department sometimes talked openly about his visits to a gay sauna down a laneway near Dublin Castle, the different practices that occurred on different floors as one went further up into the building and delved deeper into a wantonly sexual world that sounded deeply intimate and yet anonymous. In truth, there had been afternoons over the past two years when Martin was tempted to enter that sauna, not as a participant, because he had never felt any gay orientation, but as a spectator, desperate even simply to be near some sexual intimacy, as if the act of simply witnessing two strangers kissing or stroking one another might ease the loneliness he felt in his occluded position as the man who now slept alone in the attic.

Of course he never actually visited that gay club, any more than he had ever visited a prostitute or tried to pick up a strange woman in a bar. None of these acts could substitute for the feel of being held by someone you loved and who loved you. All the same, he wished that he had not witnessed these thin, young Chinese men, unselfconsciously naked as they plunged into the freezing water, their oriental features lending a girlish aspect to their buttocks. He would have been better off going to Bar Street to flounder amid strangers rather than being consumed here with a lonesomeness that he would still feel even after he flew home.

He showered and went back out to the pool reception area to examine the overpriced gifts in glass cabinets, wondering if there was anything here his daughters might like. He paused when he saw a price list on the wall, detailing a range of massages. Twice in Ireland he had endured a sports massage after his back went into spasm during his squash-playing days, but he had never had a massage abroad. He wondered if the willowy girls at reception were the masseuses. They certainly seemed to serve no other purpose. They were watching him as he studied the price list, their scrutiny so intense that he felt he needed to make conversation.

'This is where guests have a massage?' he asked, pointing down a carpeted passageway where a large sign said 'Relaxation Suite'.

'You are guest, Sir. You have massage in your room.'

'I wasn't planning to have one; I was just curious.' He felt foolish for being caught perusing the list. 'For example, what is the difference between an Asian and a Chinese massage?'

'You wait, please, Sir. The manageress must speak to you.'

Martin protested that this wasn't necessary, but the girls had already pressed a bell. Their smiles were so fixed upon him that he felt unable to leave until an older woman appeared.

'You wish massage in your room,' she said. 'I send someone now.'

'No, actually I was just inquiring about the difference between the various types.'

The willowy girls were still observing him. What he really wanted to ask was whether massages were given by them or by some burly male sumo wrestler who would crush his back. But such a question might sound seedy. The woman handed him the price list.

'Here is information,' she said. 'You pick, phone from your room.'

Martin thanked her and left. He considered sitting down in the lobby for a while, but he couldn't face the gauntlet of smiles that would await him at reception. It was safer to return to his room and pour a large drink. He lay on the bed and tried unsuccessfully to watch the propaganda on Chinese television. He switched it off and checked his email, just in case Rachel or the girls had replied. The computer gave him limited access to foreign newspaper sites, but whenever he tried to click on Google blogs his screen went mysteriously dead. This was not a country in which one could freely express an opinion.

Martin wondered if it was in a hotel like this that Chinese police recently broke down a bedroom door to beat the artist Ai Weiwei into unconsciousness and arrest him – allegedly for tax evasion – because he dared to publish on his blog a complete list of children buried alive in poorly constructed schools during the Sichuan earthquake. Two years ago Weiwei was being officially praised for his work on Beijing's 'Bird's Nest' Olympic stadium until he boycotted the opening ceremony, claiming it portrayed a fantasy version of a totalitarian state where nothing had fundamentally changed beyond its façade of new highways and skyscrapers. But the police would never have picked a hotel like this with foreign witnesses to punish someone for using blogs and twitter to puncture their carefully spun illusions. Martin would never mention dissidents like Ai Weiwei to anyone on this trip, but it was impor-tant to his soul, as against the public version of himself for hire, that he recognised – in so much as any outsider could recognise – something of the fabrication in which he was colluding.

He tried to read the briefing documents that had been prepared for tomorrow's round of meetings. He attempted to re-examine the departmental figures about his package and benefits if he too retired early, but while the numbers made financial sense his brain could just not contemplate the notion that at fifty-five his working life might be over. Across Ireland, men his age were being laid off with just statutory redundancy payments, men crippled with big mortgages who would struggle to heat their homes next winter. If he took the package, his retirement would be comfortable, but only old people retired – although he hadn't dared say that to Rachel. Maybe it was different for women who were able to fill their days with so many things, but if that Leinster schoolboy champion swimmer leaving Terenure College with such idealism could see him now, thirty-seven years on, would he regard him as someone washed up and finished who had never taken a risk? A mixture of curiosity and the need to escape from such thoughts kept drawing him back to the price-list of massage treatments, and to trying to decode what their vague descriptions actually meant.

Why shouldn't he have a massage, here alone in his room? His shoulders felt stiff, even after the swim. It would help him to sleep before the final day of meetings to come. Beijing is where you could get anything you wanted, all the guide-books said this. But what he really wanted was something that he actually only wanted in his mind. He didn't wish to start wandering down side streets where nobody spoke English, with a scam merchant on every corner, a pimp at your elbow and a begging child in your eye-line. As a younger man he had enjoyed forays into such districts, the sense of being close to danger without actually committing himself to it. But tonight he just wanted to relax and eventually sleep. He wanted the feel of a warm hand touching his skin in a safe and controlled way. It was so long since anyone touched him. On those occasions when Rachel did embrace him now, he could feel something within her push him away. Even their rare embraces had become too complicated.

'*I'm simply trying to live in the moment,*' Rachel had become fond of saying. '*You brood too much, you complicate everything. Maybe you should see a life coach to learn to live in the moment too.*'

He was still holding the printed price-list for Chinese and Asian massages and Thai foot massages. In this city where he knew no one, why complicate things by making this seem like some big decision? The Minister was in Tianjin, and Martin had spent the day drinking green tea and making meaningless conversation with minor substitutes like himself. The least he deserved was to have his shoulders rubbed down with oil. He phoned the number printed on the gym card.

'I'd like to inquire about your massages…' he began.

'You want massage?' a woman's voice replied. 'You want Nicki? You have Nicki before?'

'No. Firstly I'd like to inquire about the difference…'

'So you like Maggie then?'

'I have no experience of any of your masseuses. I'm merely…'

'I understand. No Maggie, no Nicki. We send someone, five minutes.'

The phone went dead. He could imagine Rachel laughing at him, the man able to orchestrate intergovernmental press conferences, yet unable to make himself understood by a hotel receptionist. But he realised he was probably never going to tell Rachel about this, because maybe the receptionist understood his nervous prevarication all too well from dealing with dozens of such calls. The Chinese did not do prevarication. They had their social rituals and rigid niceties, but always knew exactly what they wanted. It was one thing that travel in communist countries had taught him: everything had its exact price.

The listed prices were 350 yuan for a Chinese massage and 400 yuan for an Asian one. He would pick the Asian massage so as not to seem mean. It would be an adventure, and if the masseuse did not use too much oil his skin might not come out in a rash and Rachel need never know. Not that there was anything to know, but she might tease him when they were out with friends, making it sound different from how things really were.

The truth, however, was that he didn't know how things operated. He didn't even know what he wanted, except that he was anxious not to make a fool of himself. He poured another drink from the duty-free Baileys and walked to the window. He pondered whether he should swallow the Viagra tablet he always carried in his wallet in case Rachel's attitude changed towards him. Not that he intended anything to happen, but on the very off chance that somehow something did develop, he suddenly feared humiliation, the same loss of face that he had been cautioned never to cause to any of the Chinese officials he met.

In his case it would be less a loss of face and more a loss of virginity, because it was thirty years since his flesh had known any woman's touch except Rachel's. His diplomatic caution warned him not to take the oddly shaped tablet. The label said it did not work automatically, but only kicked in if you became aroused. However, what if he was inadvertently aroused and unable to conceal the evidence? He strongly contemplated phoning down to reception to cancel whoever was coming up. But he didn't. Instead, he stared out the full-length glass window at a hard fall of snow lying on the streets. The city out there was vast and unknowable. Maybe life was unknowable too: the way that people, relationships or marriages could subtly change. Just now his room did not feel like a luxurious hotel bedroom; it felt like a cage, cocooning him not only from the real China, but from his real life in Ireland: the life where he had once felt so secure but which now seemed to be slipping beyond his control.

The knock on the door came quicker than he had expected. Anxiously, he tidied the room. He dimmed the lights and then raised them slightly so the room didn't seem too suggestive. He considered himself in the mirror. He would never pass for distinguished looking, and needed to shave twice daily to avoid looking scruffy in afternoon meetings. His hair had flecks of grey, but at least he still possessed a full head of it and, in a certain light, retained elements of what Rachel used to call a boyish quality.

He opened the door. Thankfully, no stocky male Mongolian weightlifter stood there. He had hoped that one of the willowy girls from poolside reception might be sent up, but this woman was smaller and older and plainer looking, especially as she had her hair tied up. She possessed a nervous, anxious-to-please smile and wore a white, asexual uniform. She reminded him more of a school nurse about to give inoculation injections than his newly acquired sensual mother-in-law in Cork. Two large, striped towels were folded in her hands. She was perhaps thirty or thirty-five: Martin found it impossible to tell with Chinese people.

He said 'Ni hao,' one of the few Chinese phrases he knew. Maybe it was because his pronouncement was so poor, but the woman laughed as he stepped back to allow her to enter the bedroom. He knew immediately that this was something he could tell Rachel about, because it was as unimaginable that this woman might commit a sexual act with him as to imagine a nurse stripping off during his annual health check in the Blackrock Private Clinic. He felt oddly relieved, and was grateful he had not succumbed to adolescent fantasies by swallowing that tablet.

The woman had very limited English and Martin only knew two Chinese phrases. Twice he asked her name and twice she smiled at his atrocious attempts to pronounce it. His failure added to the comic awkwardness of the situation. They both laughed, anxious to put each other at ease. He held out the printed card that listed the treatments and pointed towards the Asian massage. She studied the card as if vaguely baffled by it and then turned to the reverse side, with the same words and prices repeated in Chinese characters. Finally she looked up.

'I understand,' she said, 'I know massage you mean.'

She turned to spread out one of her full-length towels along the bed, placing a pillow at the end. Martin knew that in a situation like this the important thing was not to lead. This was her world and not his. He liked this fact of being out of his depth. He pointed to his shirt, asking should he take it off. She smiled and nodded. He pointed to his vest and then his trousers. He had removed his shoes and socks before she arrived. Now he was just wearing a pair of black briefs. She seemed to be patiently waiting for him to remove these, amused at his shy hesitancy. He gestured towards them, with quizzical politeness.

'If like,' she said.

He removed them. She did not look at his nakedness and he did not try to hide himself as he stepped towards the bed. She pointed towards the pillow. Confused, he picked it up to cover his nakedness. She laughed and took the pillow back from him, replacing it at the head of the bed. Like a fool, he realised that this was where she wished him to place his head. It was thirty years since any woman apart from Rachel had seen him naked. He should have felt uncomfortable but he didn't. It was not just the woman's prim uniform; it was her manner. He lay face down as instructed and she placed the second long towel over him so his body was now completely covered. He could not see her; just felt her hands start to slowly massage his shoulders through the towel, and then work their way down his back.

Her hands were supple, strong without hurting him. She lowered the towel so it now covered only his buttocks and legs. He heard a squirt of oil, felt its coolness of his back and then her hands began to rub it directly into his flesh with such force that he could not prevent himself from moaning softly. It felt like she was expelling a tension trapped deep within him. He was glad that he had done nothing foolish like going to Bar Street alone. Here he felt safe with this silent woman who worked with intense concentration.

'Xie xie,' he said softly. 'Thank you. This is all the Chinese I know, "xie xie" and "ni hao".'

She laughed again softly, repeating the mispronounced words in amusement. He didn't know the etiquette for conversation with a strange woman who was massaging your naked back. It was one of the few subjects about which the civil service had yet to issue an interdepartmental memo. So he remained silent, living in the moment, to use Rachel's famous new phrase, replying only when she tried to ask him questions in her broken English. When was he leaving the hotel? Had he a wife and family?

'I have three teenage daughters,' he said. 'Two are doing their final school exams this year. They go to Loreto Dalkey.'

He knew this was a crass remark even as he instinctively said it. How could their school name possibly mean anything here, as if this woman could be expected to decipher the subtle code of social caste wrapped up in the way he defined the world of his daughters?

'I have daughter,' she replied. 'Eight-year-old. No husband. He leave when she three. Go other where.'

Martin looked back at her over his shoulder. 'I am sorry to hear that.' He spoke slowly to ensure she understood. 'Genuinely sorry.'

She nodded appreciatively. He wanted to ask more, yet didn't wish to pry into her life. But this exchange seemed to relax them, making them both parents, even if they existed in utterly separate worlds. Martin wondered about her real life at home with her daughter. How far from this hotel did she live? His translator endured a daily commute of ninety minutes just to be in the lobby in time to greet him every morning, and presumably a translator would live in a good district. At what hour did this deserted mother finish her shift, and who minded her child when she had to work late?

'Is it okay if I ask you your daughter's name?' he said.

The masseuse looked at him quizzically and then smiled when he repeated his question. She said a name proudly, but it sounded as unpronounceable as her own name had been. He tried to repeat the name however, and though he made a mess of it he knew that she appreciated him making this effort to try and connect with her.

He buried his head in the pillow then and didn't speak for a long time. He just wanted to enjoy the sensation of her hands, the way her surprising strength almost knocked the wind out of him. He felt utterly relaxed, breathing in slow, heavy breaths. And she seemed pleased that he was so appreciative, that he was willing to go with the flow and rhythm of her hands, saying nothing except, at intervals, a very soft 'xie xie,' or in English, 'thank you.'

She had been kneeling behind him, but now she came forward to stand directly in front of him so her hands could push in the opposite direction, down along his back. His head was pressed into the pillow but he could feel her short skirt touching against his hair. Her voice came from right beside his head as she knelt down so that when he glanced up their eyes were only inches apart.

'Sir? You ask for one hour. You like two hour? 800 yuan? You pay hotel, put on room?'

'Would you like that?' he asked quietly, as if this was a collective decision involving equal division of esteem.

'One hour no enough long to give proper massage.'

He wondered what pressure the hotel management exerted on their masseuses to extract this extra hour from clients. What percentage of the fee would they actually allow her to keep? Was she paid a basic retainer to cover the long hours spent waiting in some alcove downstairs in the hopes of being summoned to a bedroom, or did her sole income arise from sales commissions? Martin thought of the woman's young daughter waiting for her to come home. He contemplated her life, and his own.

'I would very much like another hour, if you are sure you can spare the time.'

The masseuse smiled, and there was something heartbreaking in the genuine relief in her features; in her gratitude at such a small favour. 800 yuan was more than Martin had intended to spend. He would need to pay for this transaction in cash so that it did not crop up on any bill after the Minister returned from Tianjin: an unnoticed incendiary device buried amid expenses that, years later, some *Sunday Independent* journalist with a fetish for the Freedom of Information Act could use to embarrass the government. He did not want it on his own credit card either, where Rachel might wonder at it. He had spent all his free time on this trip shopping for clothes and jewellery for Rachel and the girls, but this first hour tonight was his gift to himself, and now this extra hour was his gift to a single mother whose name he could not pronounce.

'Might we stop for one moment?' he asked. 'I would like to get a small drink, if that is okay.'

She seemed puzzled, but then nodded in understanding. He could not ask her to pour the drink because he did not want to appear to treat her as a maid. The only problem with needing to get up from the bed to pour his own drink was that he was naked. He wrapped the towel around him, but as he used his left hand to hold the glass, and his right hand to pour the drink, the knot came loose and the towel fell. She laughed and picked it up from the floor. It seemed silly for him to cover his nakedness again because nothing sexual permeated the atmosphere between them. He no longer felt self-conscious. This was a different culture, and what he was primarily conscious of was not his nudity, but – although unsure whether he liked this uncomfortable truth – the absolute power of his money.

What stood between him and the masseuse was not his nakedness or gender or nationality, but his wealth. He could make her night by merely paying an extra 400 yuan to a hotel who might pass on only a fraction of this to her. He walked back towards the bed and lay face down again, thanking her courteously for her patience in waiting. He took a long sip from the un-iced Bailey's as she knelt behind him again to cover up his naked back with the long towel, rearranging it so that now only his legs were exposed. She squirted oil gently onto the soles of his feet, which burnt slightly as she began to rub it into his flesh. He buried his head in the pillow to let her hands massage his soles and then the back of his calves. He knew she was deeply pleased with this extra hour's work, although it would keep her in the hotel until after midnight. Neither of them tried to speak any more. He succumbed to the deft feel of her hands, and she seemed to enjoy losing herself within her quiet concentration on the task.

Martin lost track of time, and didn't know how long had passed when a mobile phone rang. Its shrill ringtone sounded intrusive in the rich silence within the room. The masseuse stopped, with a soft, embarrassed laugh.

'It must be in your bag,' he said. 'Feel free to answer it.'

She needed to climb off the bed to quickly remove the ringing phone from her bag and glance at the flashing display panel.

'It my daughter,' she explained, as if incredulous that the child would have the audacity to disturb her in the midst of something this important.

'Please,' Martin said, 'you must answer it so.'

'This is time you pay for. I sorry; she know never phone me now.'

'I don't mind,' he said. 'The child is more important than me. She could be scared or in distress. You really must talk to her. Please, I can wait.'

'Thank you,' the masseuse said, 'xie xie. You considerate man.' She pronounced each syllable carefully, with a quiet pride in having mastered such a difficult sentence. However, she did not speak to the eight-year-old girl phoning from whatever place was home. The phone ceased ringing and she switched it off before replacing it in her bag. Silently, she resumed work on his calf muscles, but a deeper intimacy seemed to bind them: she was a mother with a child and he was a stranger with enough patience to be worried about her child; someone who viewed her as a fellow parent, sharing the same responsibilities that preoccupied him.

If they could communicate beyond the limitations of her handful of words, he would feel the need to inquire more about her daughter, and tell her something about how his twins looked identical but had utterly distinct personalities. But secretly he was relieved that this language barrier existed: it meant he did not have to make this effort. Just for once, he needn't be concerned and responsible. His career had been spent learning to put strangers at their ease, to appear to take seriously the trivial grievances of local deputations before ushering them into token meetings with higher officials. This acquired trait – this almost strangulating smoothness – had spilled over into his home life, into the ability to humour boring neighbours who whined about boundary walls; into nodding sympathetically while half listening to details of the latest feud to erupt between the warring factions who served on sub-committees in the charity Rachel was involved in; into remaining a sensitive, caring father while struggling to keep track of the array of Newpark or

Blackrock or St Andrew's boys who broke Clio's teenage heart on those occasions when she did not do the heartbreaking first.

'It's not that I don't still love you,' Rachel had said two years ago during their anniversary dinner in the Guinea Pig restaurant in Dalkey. 'It's just that I love you differently, without all that silly adolescent intensity. Our love is bound to change when we've changed. I mean, what happened to the spark you used to have when we first married, the way you could always make me laugh? No disrespect, Martin, but what made you become so dull?'

This was the anniversary dinner when she declared herself sick of returning to the Guinea Pig restaurant each year, just because he had proposed to her there, even though in the past it was Rachel who always loved his playful ritual of re-enacting his proposal at the same table every year. The night she declared that they had collectively decided not to sleep together any more, because this aspect of their marriage had reached its natural termination. The night when she hissed, 'Why do you always insist on going back over things we've already decided on?' when he replied that he had no recollection of having ever reached such an agreement. Maybe this was the irony, maybe she simply waited until he had left the room after some quarrel before making this crucial decision on behalf of them both. After all, his mid-ranking status in work meant that he was invariably absent from the room whenever real decisions of importance were made. At least he wasn't alone in having no input into decisions any more. With the Irish Cabinet literally out of the room – scattered across the globe for St Patrick's Day – the real decisions involving Ireland's fall from grace, its loss of financial sovereignty, were being taken in discreet meetings in Dublin hotels and in phone calls between the International Monetary Fund and the European Central Bank. The Minister might be in Tianjin, but the whole Cabinet could permanently migrate to China for all the impact they now exerted over their own affairs. A stage is reached in every relationship when things have gone too far to be fixed, and by now Dáil Éireann had simply become another spare bedroom in an attic.

'I became dull through having to listen to you constantly fretting about whatever mini-crisis is playing out in your mind,' he had wanted to tell Rachel on the silent drive home to Killiney after their anniversary dinner two years ago. 'Through having to sympathetically nod as you worried yourself sick about a casual remark made by some colleague in the staff room or your latest health scare, or whatever unsuitable friendship you felt one of the twins was involved in. I learnt to stay silent when I found that, no matter what words I used to try and reassure you, you automatically decided that they were the wrong words; more incriminating evidence of my insufficient sympathy for your plight. I grew quiet listening to your brain silently fret about small concerns you no longer tell me about, trivial matters that magnify in your mind because you no longer talk to me like you once did. I became dull on the day you decided that I was dull. I act dull because bubbly teenage girls need a dull father who doesn't embarrass them in front of friends by attempting to be cool. I became dull because a succession of Junior Ministers needed a dull minion to carry folders and remind them, in concise memos, about what exactly occurred in the meetings they breezed through. I surrendered my personality when it became inconvenient for too many people that I display one. But I never lost my sense of self-worth – the sense of who I truly am – until I went to kiss you tonight and your lips stiffened up to freeze me out from the intimacy we once shared.'

He said no such things on that car journey home because he recognised there were no words he could say. Rachel was facing into the menopause, with hot flushes their daughters were instructed never to mention. She was confronting the reality that certain ambitions she once nurtured would not occur. She had been a good teacher, concerned – to the point of naivety – with cherishing and encouraging each pupil. After possessing this great sense of daily purpose, and being tipped for the post of principal, she was trapped in the limbo of premature retirement. Early in their marriage she had needed Martin to be her protector, the wise companion who banished irrational fears by making her laugh, the man she could cuddle into and openly expose the labyrinth of flaws and phobias and radiance and love that held Martin mesmerised and spellbound, simultaneously exasperated and amused, made strong by her vulnerability, given fixity of purpose by the needs of her inexhaustible love.

These days he had to accept that she needed him in a different way: to be the person she could resent for whatever had not occurred in her life. In the past she had blamed herself for everything, another legacy of her relationship with a father who seemed incapable of expressing any feelings towards his daughter beyond the ability to make her feel small. Martin had learnt not to try and talk to her about this crisis in their marriage as she retreated from him into a cocoon of new friends and endless evening classes with drinks afterwards, a world where she could simply 'live in the moment' and feel good about herself. Occasionally, going into her room to kiss her goodnight, he tried to express his feelings of exclusion, but Rachel would throw her eyes to heaven and rail that she was not able to handle intense conversations at night; that he only ever brought up these things to upset her so she would not be able to sleep.

He had come to accept his demotion at home with the same stoicism with which he accepted promotions and demotions at work. His role, for now at least, was to be the man who slept in the attic, the former lover who stood in his pajamas outside what was once their bedroom door early on Sunday mornings, trying to decide whether Rachel would object to him spooning into her naked back, not wanting sex but just desperate for human warmth, for some echo of the intimacy they once shared, the sense of belonging he had taken for granted until it was suddenly withdrawn.

On some Sundays he lost the courage to turn the door handle, knowing that if he woke her she would be furious during those initial moments and he would be hurt and immediately defensive. In the terse silence, lying there, together and apart, they would be angry with each other and with themselves. On other Sundays he grew so resentful at being made to feel like a beggar that he would turn away without turning the door handle. But on occasional Sundays, when, by some miracle, he picked the right moment, just after she woke, Rachel would sleepily turn and hold him in an almost desperate embrace, like a lonely soul who had lost her way and was too scared to seek directions. There would never be sex, but the after-feel of her skin implanted on his skin made him feel alive for days to come.

Every exchange with Rachel had become layered and complicated since her retirement, every word needing to be as measured as a diplomatic dispatch for fear of causing offence. So as he spoke to this masseuse now in simple English phrases, he knew that their flawed and deeply restricted communication was still the closest he had come in two years to being his true self with anyone. He could risk being naked with her because she wanted nothing of importance. She merely wished to gain an extra 400 yuan profit for the hotel. Now Martin was fully relaxed and she seemed relaxed too, enjoying being in this huge bedroom with a man who lacked the vocabulary to be able to ask her anything of true consequence. Martin suspected that the room where her daughter awaited her return, somewhere amid the vastness of this unknowable city, was poor and cramped. But just for now both of their real lives could be suspended during this short time left before her night's work was finished.

Because he would never see the woman again, he could be totally open in his responses, could moan softly each time her hands ploughed hard into his back or caressed his knees, could surrender unselfconsciously to the warmth of her fingers. It was so long since he had felt any woman's hands on his body, much less a woman who consciously desired to please him. She did intentionally wish to please him because each time she ran her hands softly up along the back of his legs, her fingers had begun to brush faintly – faint enough to feel almost like the ghost of a touch – against the extremities of his balls hidden beneath the towel. At first he thought this was accidental because she was not actually touching his genitals. But it felt as if his testicles exercised a gravitational pull, with her fingertips feeling drawn to orbit them after each circuit of his body, softly ascending into ever closer contact with the flecks of hair that covered his balls. Each of those tiny hairs seemed to have developed a separate nerve ending, capable of yielding up previously unknown sensations. Physically the masseuse was not doing much, but she knew precisely what she was doing, and that her touch was not only pleasing him but causing the first stirrings of desire.

Then her straying hands stopped and she arranged the full-length towel so that it totally covered his nakedness again. Her hands pressed down hard through the towelling as if commencing a résumé of every region of his body she had massaged, bringing them back to the point where they had begun. His massage was over. He had endured a brush with adventure, a hint of danger, some illicit seconds that seemed about to lead to a place to which he did not know if he wished to be led. But her hands did not feel sensual any more: instead there was something almost material in their concern. Martin could imagine her drying her daughter's skin like this after an evening bath, towelling it carefully to make her feel warm and alive, singing some song to her that he could not understand.

This image made him recall his own daughters and the bliss of bathing the twins when they were small; the essence of happiness radiating from them on long-gone evenings when they and their young sister raced about naked, at three and four years old, laughing and making him laugh and feel so completely fulfilled as a person that no other world of any importance seemed to exist outside their house in Killiney. Rachel would eventually appear in the bathroom doorway to scold them about the noise, but always wound up enraptured also within that innocent magic, helping him to wrap the twins and Cliona (no thought of name changes back then, no thought that anything in their lives could ever change) in soft towels that smelt of talc and happiness.

In two days' time he would take the long flight back to that same house where nothing seemed certain any more. Before then, after tomorrow's inconsequential meetings, he would meet up with his unelectable Minister to resume his lowly place within the delegation: a nonentity masquerading as a figure of importance. But tonight, for these two hours, he had not felt like a nonentity or fraud: he had been the focus of another person's genuine courtesy and attention. The masseuse was addressing him softly. He looked back over his shoulder and smiled to thank her for her time. Then he understood that she did not just want him to rise and complete the financial formalities. She merely wished him to turn over onto his back. The massage was not actually over. She lifted up the towel to allow him to turn and he became acutely conscious of his nakedness again, but she smiled to put him at ease.

When he was settled, face upwards, she rearranged the towel neatly to cover his private parts and chest. Lying on his back meant he could watch her deft movements as she squirted oil onto the front of his legs and began to rub it in with firm deliberation. They had been silent for most of their time together but an edge was evolving within their silence now that they were face to face. Without him being able to explain exactly how it happened, their silence had assumed a conspiratorial element of unspoken expectation.

He felt in no man's land because he simply didn't know what was meant to occur. The fleetness of her swift hands aroused him, though thankfully he was disguising any physical manifestation. But her hands were becoming provocatively sensual in how they lingered for minutely longer fractions of a second at the apex of each sweeping exploration up through the downy hair along his thighs. Martin realised that he was considerably drunk from all the Baileys and so sleepy that he almost felt comatose: never more relaxed in his life and yet never more utterly alert.

Because, without warning, there were hints that this could develop into the sort of encounter he had fantasised about on lonely nights in the makeshift attic bedroom. 'You simply don't have it in you to be unfaithful, do you?' Rachel had surprised him by saying last Christmas. 'Don't take it as a criticism; it's just not in your character.' He remembered his confusion at her remark, feeling unable to decide if Rachel was praising a fundamental decency within him or expressing exasperation at his cowardice.

There was so much about the past two years he didn't even want to try and understand; clues he couldn't bring himself to piece together; an inexplicable sense that the magic that once held his world together was disintegrating. It had started with that awkward wedding in the Rochestown Park Hotel: Rachel's conservative father sitting proudly with a bride younger than his unloved daughter. Maybe this had been too much for Rachel, the father who always said he would hardly see out another Christmas suddenly enjoying a second fling at life, fuelled by Viagra and his free travel pass.

Maybe this had opened up a vista of change, reinforced her sense that life was leaving her behind, just like the loud conversations at the late-night barbecues next door used to unsettle her – neighbours boasting about Baltic investment properties and Bulgarian rental apartments they had never set foot in. Such neighbours had fallen from their perches now, made to look like fools for getting burdened with mortgages they could never repay on properties for which they had paid over the odds, having possessed no true notion of their actual worth. The way that Rachel's father now spoke so cautiously during the rare phone calls to his daughter made him also sound trapped, as if his new wife were standing beside him, ready to censor his words. Martin suspected that his father-in-law was – if not unhappy – then certainly fearful of the changed reality of his altered life. Perhaps the doctor had married foolishly, but at least he took a risk. Martin remembered Rachel's words: 'Say what you want about my father, but he's no pushover. He's a real man.'

Why was Martin so scared of risk and change, perpetually trying to hold back time? Everything changes: men change, women change, girls change and become women. He remembered the night he heard voices and music from Clio's bedroom, with Clio and Simon Doran from Dalkey – her official Junior Cert study-buddy, as she termed the teenage boy – laughing at their own attempts to hold a halting conversation in French a week before they were due to do their aural test. Clio's bedroom had gone so silent that after a time Martin presumed the youngsters had gone out. He had pushed open Clio's door half an inch to discover how the aural had turned oral, to witness how his youngest daughter, with a blasé lack of haste, was matter-of-factly sucking the teenager's cock. Clio had her back turned to the door, the upper slopes of her buttocks shockingly visible as she knelt in low-slung jeans. He had longed to call out her name in distress – not 'Clio' but 'Cliona,' his little Cliona. Instead, he had said nothing, just furtively stepped back from the door and retreated downstairs on tiptoes.

Starting the car, he had driven a hundred yards up the road towards the park with the obelisk at its summit, in the opposite direction to the one

Simon Doran would take. Martin had sat there, watching in the rear-view mirror until the boy left the house, because he could not bear to be present in his own home while this was occurring, yet there was nowhere else he was meant to be. A real man would have gone into his daughter's bedroom and caused a row, but Martin had never even informed Rachel. Rachel's mood swings were so extreme that he hadn't known whether she would be shocked or merely say, 'that's perfectly normal,' as if this was another example of him over-complicating life.

Clio's friends casually referred to this sexual feat as a 'BJ,' reducing an intimate act – which once seemed so promiscuous that he had rarely persuaded Rachel to perform it during all their years of marriage – into a throwaway abbreviation, a handy bailout alternative for shy girls when confronted with their inability to hold a proper conversation with a boy. There were so many new terms – 'study buddies,' 'fuck buddies,' 'friends with benefits' – all now common currency in a new Ireland he had missed out on, an Ireland Rachel seemed *au fait* with since abruptly announcing the termination of their physical marriage. Those odd lives that strangers inhabited – a twilight landscape of internet meeting-sites. Did all this illicit coupling actually occur in hotel bedrooms, or was it just stories concocted by middle-aged women confiding in packs at the revolving carousel bar in the Leopardstown Inn – spinning fantasies about alleged friends of friends, like his classmates once spun fantasies about imaginary sexual exploits a lifetime ago in Terenure College, blurring the distinctions between reality and wish fulfilment.

But the hands of this masseuse were so real that Martin wished they would never stop. 'Xie xie,' he said so softly he could not tell if she heard. He had no idea if she could follow his confession that followed: 'It is so long since any woman touched my body. I am not a bad man, but I am a deeply lonely one.'

She smiled at him but did not try to reply. Was her life lonely too, abandoned by her husband, left to raise his child? How long would it take her to get home tonight to whatever small room she lived in? He could envisage her, after finishing her work with him, descending into the bowels of this hotel where the illusion of glamour ended and the corridors became functional. He could see her changing from this anaemic white uniform to become somebody different, part of the other China that it was impossible for him to know. They would return to vastly different worlds after leaving the artificial cocoon of this luxurious room, but he knew that a bond existed between them at this moment, with their outside lives suspended. Both were enjoying this creative ambiguity, the uncertainty as to what the next step would be, the foreignness of each other. She might never stay as a guest in a bedroom as lavish as this, but he was the true outsider here as her straying hands marked out her territory. He was a visitor with no demands or preconceptions, willing to be led or not led, to allow this massage end at whatever juncture she decided upon.

In addition to being drunk he knew that the time difference still made everything disconcerting, but it felt as if decades of responsibilities were being rubbed away by that oil. He was suddenly his true self again: a man unburdened by a thousand cares, not always torn in two by trying to please warring factions. Before he met Rachel – before he became absorbed in her perpetual need for reassurance – he had left himself open to every experience. A good Leaving Certificate had led him, almost inadvertently, into the public service, after his mother pestered him into applying. He had never intended to stay for more than a year or two. He had been going to become a nomad without possessions or ties, leaving himself open to the full possibilities of experience.

Martin stood out during his early years within the department by his defiant unconventionality. He was the office joker, the rebel standing up to the slimy Higher Executive Officer whose groping hands made too free with new girls still on probation. The department had owned his body from nine to five, but his spirit was unassailably his own. Some Friday evenings he used to give his week's wages to the homeless tramp who had constructed a makeshift wigwam amid foliage on a canal bank outside the office, because it felt right to do so and Martin wanted to genuinely experience hunger for the rest of the week. On other weekend nights he went walking to the Wicklow mountains from his flat in Rathgar, purely so as to savour the exhausted exhilaration of watching dawn unfold over the city beneath him.

He was a different person before he met Rachel, but he had been desperately lonely also. This memory is what kept him in his marriage now when Rachel's love was no longer obvious. Often he told himself that he was hanging in there for Clio and Aisling and Aoife's sake, so they would not need to choose sides amid the fragmentation of separation. At other times he pretended that he was enduring this limbo for Rachel's sake, because – beneath her new indifference – she still needed him, even if only as someone to blame. In truth, though, he remained tucked within the niche of marriage for his own sake: scared that he would be unable to cope with the loneliness of being on his own.

His occasional longings to leave his marriage were as much a fantasy as his talk had been, during the early years, of leaving the shelter of the civil service to become that free-spirited nomad he longed to be as a boy, exploring the limits of foreign cities. Martin needed to be needed. He needed a function. He needed to wait among the line of wary fathers in cars, picking up their underdressed daughters outside the Wes disco. He needed to be the safe pair of hands to whom his superiors could entrust the most skittish Junior Minister; the sensible colleague his peers could discreetly phone for advice; the decent soul who had made his true nature vanish into the black hole of his seemingly indisputable goodness because this was the safest place on earth in which to hide.

But he wasn't saintly or good – even if, in the scale of life's sins, he was not entirely bad. He had desires and fantasies and moments of rage about slights at work or at home that he was careful never to let his colleagues or daughters see. Some evenings, stuck in rush hour traffic alone on the Rock Road, he would hurl the vilest abuse at the long snake of motorists in front of him. On some rainy nights when he risked letting the family dog off the lead in Killiney Hill Park he would kick the ageing mutt if he got lost among the trees and emerged, in answer to Martin's angry calls, tail down and shaking. Maybe this was why Rachel's feelings towards him had changed: his efforts to be nice to everyone else left him so drained that sometimes, in exhaustion, he would snap at her when he reached home because by then he had simply nothing left to give to anyone.

Tonight, however, in this foreign hotel he could simply be himself at last: a middle-aged naked man stretched out beneath a towel, which barely concealed the evidence that he currently possessed a fifty percent deposit on an erection. Here he needed to be nobody's rock; there was nowhere to hide. And this woman with her unpronounceable name knew exactly what his desires were. Her fingers stopping their slow stroking of his thigh, she looked directly at him. Her hands make a discreet and friendly gesture towards the towel covering his groin.

'You like I massage you there?' she asked quietly.

'I would like that very much.'

She smiled. 'You give me tip?'

'What size tip would you like?'

She blushed bashfully and he smiled because the situation seemed vaguely absurd. Reflecting back over the evening, this was the obvious moment it had been building to, but for him in his fifty-five-year-old innocence there was nothing obvious about it. Beijing might be the city where you could buy everything, but she was a masseuse employed by a respectable five-star hotel, summoned on room service. Throughout his stay in China he was told to constantly barter. Whenever traders approached him, his translator would launch into fevered, seemingly bad-tempered disputes with them. This savage haggling could seem to be about to result in blows, before the screaming matches ended with satisfied smiles as quickly as they began.

But this service was not a pair of shoes for Rachel or jewellery for his daughters. How could you barter about something so intimate? How could you put a price on a service when you were not even sure what you wanted or what was on offer? Perhaps this was what he had been secretly hoping for, but there was a vast chasm between fantasy and actuality. If the woman had made such an offer at the start of his massage, then decency or cowardice or whatever brand of moral integrity Martin still clung to would have led him to politely decline. But that was before her hands had reminded him of how a woman's hands felt. She had allowed him the time to relax and escape from his real life and he knew that he did not want this interlude to stop. With consummate diplomatic skill she had steered events and circumstances, and now he wanted her to continue taking the lead.

'You must tell me what size tip you want,' he said quietly.

She shook her head and gave an embarrassed laugh.

'No, you must tell tip you wish give.'

'You have to guide me here. What tip would you like? Please, I genuinely know nothing about these things.'

A note of playfulness remained between them, but it was infused with tension. They were both professional negotiators, sufficiently professional not to want to lose the human bond between them. They were being exceedingly polite, but behind their politeness they were trying to establish each other's bottom line. Not that Martin wished to exploit her – indeed he was uncertain whether he was exploiting the woman or the woman was exploiting him – but, while wanting to be generous, he did not wish to pay a vastly inflated price for her, as yet unspecified, services.

'No,' she insisted politely, 'it you must tell what tip you wish give.'

He understood – or thought he understood – her moral logic. For her to suggest a price was akin to actively selling herself. Legally, within the hotel, this might be forbidden, though he could hardly imagine guests complaining at the front desk about overcharging. When being briefed for this trip, he was repeatedly told how important it was for the Chinese never to lose face. This was as true for a single mother with nothing to sell except her hands as for any of the official delegations he had met. Therefore it was a delicate negotiation, although he had no training in how to progress it.

'What might make you go home feeling good about yourself?' he asked.

He knew this was an odd choice of words and also partly dishonest. Martin wanted her to feel good about herself, but mainly so that he could feel good about himself for having made her feel valued. He wanted this parity of esteem because it was what his training had taught him to always seek to achieve: a compromised outcome where everybody walked away feeling they had achieved something

'You give hotel 800 on room bill,' she said. 'Now maybe give something just me, in US dollars cash.'

'I have no dollars,' he explained. 'I only have euros.'

She looked perplexed by this foreign word, as if ill versed in the exchange rate of the euro. This was another thing that travel in communist countries had taught him: American dollars were the only currency by which people seemed utterly mesmerised.

'There are nine hundred and twenty yuan in a hundred euros,' he explained. 'So help me here. Be my guide. What would you truly like?'

Her laugh was girly and truly embarrassed. 'What I like?' She seemed perplexed by the odd question, as if nobody had ever asked her this in her life. 'What I like two, three hundred dollars.' She said this amount wildly as if it was a fortune beyond comprehension, but also in a way that suggested she had been deeply hurt in the past by derisory offers, by indifference and rejection and rudeness, by the abrasive arrogance of rich men in rooms like this. Martin's erection had wilted. He felt less drunk now and desperately wished that this encounter had ended when he thought it was over, after she replaced the towel full length on his back. But it was ongoing and, although deeply awkward, this was the closest he had come to touching a woman in so long.

'As a gift I will leave one hundred and fifty euro on the dressing-table,' he said, expecting her to look pleased. But she went silent as if hurt. She glanced away and then looked back at him. For the first time he noticed that there was something of Aisling in her eyes. He cursed himself that, at this moment of all moments, he was being reminded of his own daughter and how he would hate Aisling to ever find herself in a situation like this.

'You give hotel 800, but me only 150,' she said quietly.

'Not yuan,' he explained, 'your tip is in euro: the currency of the European Union. On the dressing-table I leave you two hundred euro… no, two hundred and fifty euro. That is worth more than two thousand yuan. It is all the foreign currency I have in my wallet. Is that okay?'

Hesitantly, as if still confused, she nodded. She seemed so unsure that he sensed her evenings did not always end like this. Could this possibly be her first time to offer such a service? Had the intimacy that developed between them led her into uncharted waters? But then he dismissed this idea, because in the space of a few moments – through that hurt look in her eyes, her seeming vulnerability and his guilt at being reminded of Aisling – her tip had grown in value to beyond the three hundred dollar fortune mentioned with such childish awe. Martin realised why he remained a mid-ranking civil servant: out in the real world he would make as lousy a negotiator as his neighbours had proven to be when buying foreign property. He had offered more than he could afford or she could have possibly expected, yet she still looked vaguely dissatisfied.

'We have to take our time; you must give me time… to be ready,' he said. 'How long will you stay?'

'My daughter waiting. I can stay one half hour.'

He rose from the bed and took his wallet from his suit trousers. He entered the bathroom as if to check his money, but in reality it was to take the Viagra tablet secreted away there. Not that he had needed Viagra when his lovemaking with Rachel was naturally intertwined within their lives. He would not have needed it now either if their massage had continued in its original, sensual, unhurried way. But the interruptions and negotiations, his annoyance at having probably overpaid and the intrusive thoughts that kept bringing everyday reality flooding back meant that he needed it because all the sexual drive seemed drained from his body. The problem with Viagra was that it took twenty minutes to work. He should explain to the woman what he had taken, but this would only make his embarrassment worse. Not only would he be scared of being unable to perform – even though he merely needed to lie there and relax – but, in this of all countries, he was now scared of being the one to lose face.

He walked from the bathroom naked: it felt foolish to still wear a towel. He poured himself another large Baileys and offered her one. She smiled appreciatively but refused. He offered her anything from the minibar – tea or coffee, water or fruit – but she just laughed at his prevarication and put her arms around him in a playfully affectionate hug. He knew now she was exhilarated about her tip: she must have properly calculated the exchange rate while he was in the bathroom. His briefing notes for tomorrow's meetings stated that the average annual industrial wage in Beijing was eight thousand dollars. He had just paid her more than two weeks' wages for a half hour of unspecified work. He drained the Baileys and turned to her.

'Please,' he asked softly, 'will you take off your uniform?'

She nodded but her eyes seemed unsure. Was this part of the deal, within the parameters of her work? But maybe there were no fixed rules, about this or anything else in life; maybe this had always been his mistake. Maybe they would simply have to invent their own rules. He had paid her but did not own her, any more than his jumped-up Junior Minister owned him. He undid the first two buttons of her blouse. She acquiesced, her shy, tentative look reminding him of girls in bedsits decades ago. When he reached for the third button she stayed his hand and he accepted that this was as far as she was willing to go. But then he realised that she feared his clumsy fingers might damage the buttons, the remainder of which she undid with swift gracefulness. Her bra had the image of a butterfly embroidered on the left cup. Her breasts were truly beautiful. Oddly he felt no lust, just a sense of wonder. How long was it since he undressed any girl? Since long before

Rachel, because Rachel had never been a girl you could undress. Did boys do this with Aisling and Aoife? He didn't want to think about that because, just at that moment, he didn't feel like a father or a husband any more: he felt strangely alive and peculiarly alone.

The masseuse stepped back. She removed her skirt with one neat motion and carefully folded it with the top half of her uniform on the chair. He sat naked on the edge of the bed and she stood before him. She must have discreetly undone the bra strap at the back because he was able to put his hand inside the bra cups and draw out her left breast. The nipple was long and different to any nipple he had previously seen in the flesh. He stared at it in boyish wonder and looked up at her face.

'It's beautiful,' he said. 'You are truly beautiful.'

'No beautiful.' She blushed. 'Ordinary. I ordinary.'

'No,' he insisted. 'Beautiful.'

She could not disguise her genuine pleasure at his words. Martin knew that this exchange at least between them was real. In her other life a young man had deserted her, leaving her with a daughter. What type of life did a deserted mother lead in China? He wanted to ask her this question, but most of all he wanted to keep touching her breasts. She acquiesced again, turning the angle of her body slightly so that he could see her small, delicate buttocks, barely covered by panties.

'Beautiful,' he repeated. He wanted to use other terms to describe her but knew that she would not understand them. He wasn't even sure if she understood the simple words he was using but she understood their tone and seemed genuinely moved by his wonder, her pleasure manifesting itself in girlish embarrassment. He was good at making people feel good, and sensed that it was a long time since anyone had made her feel this appreciated. She stood uncertainly before him and Martin was uncertain as to what was allowed and what was not. He knew he did not want to have actual sex with her and be unfaithful to Rachel. He had given this woman money to be his pleasure thing, but now what he most wanted was to give her pleasure. It was the ridiculous notion, as if she was the guest and he the underling. But he took her breast in his mouth to kiss it and suck upon its sweetness and when he looked up to smile at her she smiled back.

Then she softly pushed him backwards onto the bed. She lay beside him, with her naked breasts against his chest, and he heard a new sound, a feline purring, come from her mouth. This sound was bogus and intrusive: it belonged to the backing track of badly dubbed porn movies. She was making these noises of female abandon to try and please him, but he knew also that they were forming a wall of sound to keep him at bay. Her body and her mind had gone into neutral and he realised that nothing about this moment was real or genuine any more. She had ceased to be a masseuse, a single mother supporting a child at home. She had become a hooker, even though he felt certain she was no hooker. It was as if she was trying to decipher what persona he wished her to inhabit, and then transform herself into his fantasy. Was this who she was really was? Was everything that had previously occurred between them just an act?

Her breasts and belly rubbed against his body, working hard to try to excite him. Her hands offered to do whatever he wished them to do, but what he truly wanted was for her to stop uttering these horrendous fake moans. He could find no way to ask this without insulting her and halting the awkward flow of this messy and already fatally interrupted business. While he had been allowed to ask her to remove her clothes, he could not ask her to remove her final defence from being truly naked: this shield of fake sound. Her hand strayed to his penis, which had not yet managed to grow erect. It was too soon for the Viagra to kick in, and her simulated moans had destroyed any true intimacy or desire. He felt marooned between paradise and hell.

'Could you kiss me here?' He pointed to his nipples and she kissed them compliantly, her tongue encircling them. She moved her hand away from him, and he heard a squirt of oil before her fingers returned to his barely erect penis. The oil made her caressing palm so soft that, within seconds, he had come in a soundless anticlimax, bereft of the slightest pleasure or relief. He patted her heavily lacquered hair and she recognised this as a sign to be still. They lay together on the bed. He reached out for her and she hugged him. Then, when his grip weakened, she lifted herself away and disappeared into the bathroom.

She returned with a small pile of tissues. Softly, she cleaned away whatever seed had splashed onto his midriff until no evidence existed that any mishap had occurred. She observed him closely, concerned at his lack of pleasure. She seemed like a girl again, anxiously needing some praise or acknowledgement.

'Xie xie,' he said quietly. 'Thank you.'

But there was something different in his tone, drained of emotion. It was over, the betrayal – there was no other word for it – which he had often fantasised about in the loneliness of his attic bedroom. His fall had been as abrupt and humiliating as the fall of Ireland. Now he felt fragile and vulnerable and wanted to be alone. The memory of her artificial moans mocked him. But was her purring more fake than anything else that occurred here? Had this sense of a growing bond been merely in his head, his fantasy that they were linked by being parents of daughters in two different worlds?

None of this was the masseuse's fault: she had made those moaning noises in an attempt to excite him, to become whatever compliant version of a fantasy woman she felt he wished her to be. Maybe other men were turned on by the pretence that she was in heat, as insatiable as a porn actress in a bad film. The masseuse – if this indeed was the correct term for her – had merely been trying to conform to his fantasy and emotionally retreat from whatever acts were required to feed her daughter. That is, if she actually possessed a daughter, if one single word she had uttered since entering his room was real. Why should it be real, when she could logically presume that foreign men in rooms like this, who surely possessed unimaginable wealth in her eyes, were bound to lie to her?

His penis felt numb. Already, what had just occurred no longer felt real. It would only be real when he could think properly about it alone. Martin disentangled himself from her arms and walked to the safe located inside the wardrobe. The important thing now was for no trace of this transaction to appear on his bill. But could he trust her enough to give her eight hundred yuan in cash to pay the hotel? When he turned around he saw that, in the few moments it took him to count out the money, she had slipped back into her uniform. She looked utterly different, sitting on the side of the bed. There was no fake gaiety, no girlish laughter. She looked tired after her long evening. He approached, his movements circumspect, as if terminating a formal meeting. The etiquette when you paid for any transaction in China was to hold out the bank notes with both hands to show that it was a sum worthy of respect. He quietly counted out two hundred and fifty euros and placed it with both hands on the bed beside her.

'This is for you,' he said. 'Thank you.'

She looked down at the banknotes, then up at him. She nodded in gratitude. Chinese etiquette meant that people tried to convey little in facial expressions for fear of losing face, or causing others to lose face. But the relief in her smile suggested that other men had not always paid what they promised, and that she found this moment awkward too. He didn't like himself for already starting to calculate how much he had overpaid her: two weeks' wages in Chinese terms for a few unfulfilled seconds. Tonight had been a lesson in the difference between reality and fantasy. Maybe the past giddy decade had been the same for Ireland. For him this loss of control would never reoccur because, even if tempted, he had sold his innocence and understood the emptiness of having purchased something you didn't actually want merely because you could.

Perhaps if they had waited until the Viagra kicked in and there had been a surge of genuine pleasure he might not feel so bereft. But pleasure – or the lack of it – was incidental to his betrayal and his fall. There was no other word for it, like there was no other word for the fall of Ireland – despite government delegations still going hither and thither to dispense shamrock to foreign heads of state, like back in the days when Ireland was a sovereign state not being run from the Dublin hotel bedrooms where the advance guard from the IMF were now gathered with calculators, taking conference calls. Ireland had been busted by banks and developers; by political parties hell-bent on outdoing each other in dispensing largesse to voters who had come to expect largesse – everyone locked in a giddy fantasy that could only have ended in a fall.

Martin felt sick and empty now, but maybe this was how the solicitor who lived next door to them felt every morning when he woke and realised that, drunk on the power of simply being able to, he had paid vastly over the odds for properties that were now worthless. Over the past year Martin had felt a certain smugness at being the only person on his estate not to own at least one rental property. He had avoided the investment clubs friends had been sucked into that were essentially pyramid scams. Yet all his outward probity was just a sham if his marriage, the very core of his soul, was now as bogus as the fake wealth that his neighbours had flashed over the past decade.

In the past half hour he had betrayed the two most important people in his life. Not the present day Rachel who had declared their physical marriage to be over. This new Rachel was wrapped up in her menopause and sweats and mood swings and texting friends from her off-limits bedroom in the Killiney house that would soon be too big for them once the girls moved out and silence reigned. There was another Rachel he had betrayed: the tender, innocent girl with whom he first fell in love and whom he still desperately loved. Even if this vanished Rachel no longer existed, she would still have been deeply wounded by his actions tonight.

Just as importantly, he had betrayed himself, the young man whom this original Rachel had loved. No matter how he dressed up tonight; no matter how many drinks were consumed, or how lonely he had felt so far from home on this meaningless junket, or how lonely he would still feel once he returned home, he had stained his own integrity, the moral codes by which he once lived. The price he paid the Chinese woman was unimportant because no sum could ever buy back his integrity. All the same, it was vital to leave no trace of this transaction anywhere, except on his soul. Therefore, holding the money solemnly with both hands, he risked also placing 800 yuan down on the bed beside her.

'Please,' he asked, 'can you also pay the hotel for me?'

She understood his words and recognised also that he trusted her. The masseuse nodded. She placed both sets of banknotes carefully on top of her towels and then folded over the towel so that no trace of money remained between them. She could leave now but seemed reluctant to do so.

'You have ten minutes left,' she said. 'I promised stay one half hour. I give head massage.'

He didn't want a head massage; he wanted to be alone. But he felt that she needed their last physical contact to be a non-sexual one so as to allow her to slip back into her original role. She sensed his reluctance, but he yielded and lay face up on the bed, staring at the ceiling. She knelt at the end of the bed, fingers pressing hard on his temples. The sensation was nice, but he could not relax now. He felt trapped: unable to see what she was really doing because he could not turn his head to look back. He tried to remember where he had left his wallet, his BlackBerry smartphone and his passport. He could not imagine her stealing from him, yet this exchange of money had changed everything between them. It was hard to believe that just a few moments ago she had lain naked beside him, with Martin touching her breasts, overawed at this glimpse into a forbidden world from which he had always shied away, a world where nothing was off limits, where the only barriers existed in your wallet and your conscience. But this world did not speak to him of freedom any more; it had at its core a void of loneliness.

Was this woman lonely? Was that why she was putting off her return to the Spartan basement where she would shed this white uniform and become someone else, starting the long trek home to where her child would have fallen asleep. Martin accepted that he would never be sure of anything about her except that she wished him to relax now. She did not want to leave him feeling so uneasy. She wanted to please him and then to go and so, for her sake, he closed his eyes and tried to relax. Even though his eyes were closed, he sensed her face draw near to his. Her voice was beguiling.

'Tomorrow night, you like I give massage again?'

'No, thank you.'

'Tomorrow night come back.'

He opened his eyes, glad not to have to look up into her eyes because she moved her head back. 'I'm afraid I have no money left,' he explained.

This was a lie, and she knew it was a lie because western men always have money left. They have credit cards and electronic methods of summoning cash whenever cash is needed. But it was a lie he was sticking to, though she softly asked him again and again, while stroking his temples, if he might not summon her tomorrow night, no matter how late, even just for one hour, just for a simple massage. She sounded jaded now. This head massage had not been to relax him but to tout for more business. Yet he did not blame her – this was her only chance to make her pitch and not be dependent on the mood of the manageress who answered the phone tomorrow night and could coldly pick any one of the other girls anxiously awaiting work. All this mother had left to sell was her hands, and she was doing this in the only manner she knew how.

Both she and Martin were hustlers. He would spend all day tomorrow trying to sell Ireland in whatever manner he could to the delegations the embassy had him lined up to meet. Everyone in this hotel was hustling for something – from international trade concessions to cheap Thai massages, from building contracts for skyscrapers to hasty handjobs. The only difference was that, as you rose higher in the chain, you could cloak your naked pitch in diplomatic niceties, dress it up with advisors and minions. He raised his two hands to gently touch her wrists as a sign to cease massaging his head. She held his hands for one moment.

'It okay,' she said quietly. 'I know you will no phone, but I like you… you make me feel good. You nice man; not all man I meet nice.'

He stood up, conscious that he was only wearing underpants.

'It was nice to meet you,' he said. 'Thank you for your time.'

'If you change mind, I want you know I here all night tomorrow,' she said. 'I will not tell my name because you no remember it, but please, just in case change your mind, write my number. If you phone and ask for number, they know you want me.'

Her words struck him as the saddest speech imaginable: her whole identity reduced down to a number. He wrote the three digits on the notepad on his desk, knowing that he would take this back to Ireland as a reminder nobody else could ever decode.

'I wish you well,' he said with a slight bow. 'I hope life works out well for you and for your daughter.'

He put his hand out and shook hers. The gesture seemed ridiculously formal. Maybe he wanted to maintain a diplomatic distance, or simply to give her his full respect. He did not know if she understood all his words, but she seemed to understand his tone and be pleased that he acknowledged her child. Holding the folded towels carefully, she went to leave. But then, when she had the bedroom door open, she placed the towels down for a moment in the corridor and ran back inside the room to hug him. She kissed him quickly, almost furtively, fully on the lips, and he felt sure that this was no hustle; it was her parting gift to him, a tiny glimpse into her core. Before he could respond she ran back into the corridor. Picking up the folded towels, which betrayed no hint of what they held, she was gone, shutting the door behind her.

Martin stood there for an indefinite time, staring at the closed door, surprised by this unexpected kiss. His lips felt different from the rest of his body: the only part of him not numb. Finally he walked across to the full-length window to pull open the curtains. He was on the fourteenth floor. The world spread out beneath him, cold and vast and unreachable. Beijing's traffic had finally quietened down. On every side, skyscrapers was going up, a barometer of the shift in global power. The Irish builders who had caused the fall of their own country were now here hustling for work: minor whores, bit-players but bit-players in a massively unfolding jigsaw. There were contracts to be won in China for office complexes, conference centres, apartment blocks teeming with lives he would never connect to, trapped here in his luxury prison where real communication was impossible.

Had anyone he met in the past five days shown him their true face? His translator? The driver supplied by the embassy, but undoubtedly vetted by the Chinese? Perhaps this masseuse was the only person to actually expose anything of themselves. He did not mean her breasts or even her sad hustle for extra work at the end. During most of their time together she had striven to act out a role for him, but he still needed to believe that, if only for occasional brief seconds, they had connected in ways that were tangible.

Was it the moment when she blushed – genuinely embarrassed – at seeing him overawed by his first sight of her breasts? Her pleasure had been real – not when he sucked at them, unable to prevent himself – but when he gazed up into her eyes to brush away her protestations that her breasts were merely ordinary. She had also been touched earlier – he felt sure of this – when he tried to persuade her to answer the phone call from her daughter. She had not understood all his words; but understood his willingness to be patient.

What he would never be certain of was whether her parting kiss was for real. Was this to thank him for wishing her and her daughter well, or merely a final, desperate tout for business? Why did it need to have been one thing or the other? Maybe nothing in life was black and white, fully real or illusionary? Maybe Rachel did still love him, but in a way that she could not openly express any more. Martin was relieved that the masseuse was gone, yet felt homesick and desperately lonely. He wished that he had not felt so detached from the woman at the end. But after he came – in so much as you could call it a climax – he had felt detached even from himself, as if the entire world was suddenly smaller and squalid and deflated, as if he was dead already and this had been the ghost of the distant memory of a climax from some precious life.

Would it feel more real in retrospective if they had waited for the Viagra to work, if he had grown so rock hard that it took him a lifetime to come? He didn't think so, because while the woman's breasts had undoubtedly been real as she lay beside him, already the whole experience felt unreal like it belonged to a story told to him by someone else in a bar, another traveller's tale about how a naked single mother had once softly cupped a stranger's testicles in an anonymous hotel bedroom.

This scared him: it suggested that the most frightening thing about infidelity was that there was nothing memorable about it at all. Behind all the fuss and broken vows, maybe it was so humdrum as to be instantly forgettable. He wondered if death would be equally forgettable, a damp squib beneath all the mystery and symbolism in which people wrapped it up, despite the way people mentally spent their whole lives preparing for it. Maybe death was also mundanely accomplished in a second, with the rest of humanity sweeping onwards, barely noticing your absence? He wondered if the masseuse believed in some form of afterlife. It would have been a curious question to ask. He might have truly glimpsed her naked then, in a rare moment of exposure, if she had answered honestly, with no way of knowing what reply would best please the customer who was paying for her time.

He would never know what she truly thought because he had never properly seen her. She could have made a good civil servant: looking back, he realised that she understood how pliability gave you the power of invisibility; how – by becoming what other people wished you to be – you could appear to be present while not truly being there. Then the thought occurred – and this thought scared him – that perhaps he really did not know Rachel either, and not only since her retirement, when her attitude towards him changed.

Maybe he had never truly known his wife. Maybe even in the early years, when it seemed that no two people could ever be so close, when she had confided in him about every fear and memory from her childhood, maybe, consciously or subconsciously, she was acting out a part without being aware of it. Maybe she was always so busily striving to be the person that she thought he wanted her to be, the wife, mother and teacher she felt she should strive to be, that one morning when she woke to find herself classified as retired, she simply stopped trying. Maybe she had woken up to realise that all reality is essentially fake. Maybe she had said: *I will continue to act out this dutiful fantasy in front of neighbours and friends. I will even fool myself into believing it in public. But in private, when we are alone, I refuse to pretend to be someone that I can no longer be any more.*

Had anything about the past quarter of a century of Martin's life been real? Did he truly know who any of his daughters was? Certainly he had known them when they were small and needed a protective daddy, like all young girls do. But the three of them had only been embryonic then, lost in the make-believe of My Little Pony and Happy Families, just setting forth on their journey to become adolescents who got straight A grades and cut themselves. Now they were grown women in all but name, with women's bodies and desires, whether he liked this or not. On some sofa in some front room in Dalkey, one of the twins might now be giving a boy the pleasure that this nameless woman had tried to give Martin. Or maybe they engaged in acts ten times more shocking – shots of vodka, lines of cocaine, silk scarves tied to bedposts, camera-phones running as they obligingly looked up and laughed for some private video, with cum smeared on their faces.

He didn't want to think such terrible thoughts, but could not stop the most explicit images from entering his mind. The truth was that he could stop or change nothing about their futures. The girls would go their own way and, in time, Rachel might go her way too after he also took the retirement package and they were thrust together day and night. Seizing the pension pot on offer was the only logical thing to do for anyone in his suddenly obsolete generation of civil serv-ants and public service workers: the people who had eschewed risk from an early age, certain that they knew how their futures would turn out. But the future was not a country that he knew any longer, and he did not possess the tools to fix the past – the tiny, incremental mistakes and rows that had gradually turned Rachel against him. Throughout his life he had made the mistake of playing it safe: trying to do the right things and be the kind of man that he felt the people who relied upon him needed him to be. He had seen himself as their rock, but really he was just a stag-ing post in their lives, a booster rocket that falls away after carrying a space capsule as high as it can, and then gets burnt up upon re-entering the atmosphere.

Martin felt lost at this hotel window, but also oddly resigned to his fate and relieved to rec-ognise the fact that the people whom he truly loved and had spent his life trying to nurture possessed this right to outgrow him and physically and emotionally leave him behind. What time was it now in Ireland? He tried to imagine his detached house on that small estate on top of Killiney Hill, which got cut off from the outside world every time it snowed. In two days' time he would attempt to fit back inside that fractured world. He would arrive home with the requested Ugg boots for his girls, the dutiful husband and father bearing jewellery and silk scarves and trinkets.

But he would be essentially a stranger because his family were becoming strangers to him. He tried to imagine their faces, but felt too exhausted to visualise them. The Minister and senior officials were in Tianjin, consuming Cognac and concocting a narrative to justify the vast expense of this trip, to sell it to the national press and the Cabinet when the Minister reported back. Tomorrow Martin would shadow-box his way through his final unimportant meetings, the loose ends he had been entrusted to tie up. He would also concoct reports about their successful outcome, swallow his own lies and sell himself short by avoiding the truth that this entire trip, like almost everything he had done in his career over the decades, was a monumental waste of time.

But those lies and three-card-trick illusions could wait for tomorrow. His reflection in this hotel window left nowhere to hide. If a passer-by glanced up from the street, Martin would resemble an insect stuck to the glass, the pinned specimen of a middle-aged foreigner growing older. That was the only unadorned truth that he could say about himself: he was a man, naked except for a pair of black briefs, imperceptibly ageing at a plate glass window.

He closed his eyes and suddenly became scared to open them again. It made no sense but Martin became frightened that somehow the next thirty years might have already passed, with this huge window having shrunk down to just one small glass pane. A voice whispered in his head that he was merely yet again reliving some night from long ago; that Rachel was long since dead, if he could only remember; and his daughters had emigrated to new, unimaginable lives. Martin knew that none of this was true. He was only fifty-five years old, but the whispering voice scared him so much that he felt too frightened to open his eyes. The voice told him that he had reached the lonesome moment he had spent his whole life dreading: the moment when nobody who remained in that government department remembered his name, when everything about him was being wiped away, including his own shit and piss after he soiled himself, including his dignity and identity and his last remaining handful of confused memories. The whisperer intimated that life only felt truly real when nothing was real any longer; it only made sense when nothing made sense, when he could scarcely remember his name or the fact that he had once been a husband and father. Only then, when there was no future, would the past begin to make sense, during his few lucid moments like this when he could look back and recognise his life's true pattern.

Martin told himself again that all this was crazy: with luck he still had another thirty years to live. He knew who he was: a mid-ranking civil servant about to join his wife in early retirement before his pension was cut. If he would just open his eyes this reality would be confirmed. But he kept his eyes shut because, in this state of drunkenness or exhaustion or inner revelation, he knew that he was more than merely an ageing man with his hands pressed against a hotel window: in his core he retained the essence of every person whom he had been during every stage of his life. He was still the shy champion swimmer growing up in Terenure, the youth who walked up into the Wicklow Mountains at night to witness the spectacle of dawn, the young lover first kissing Rachel outside a pub in St Stephen's Green, the father cradling his first- and second-born (with only one minute between them) and experiencing such a protective love that he immediately knew he would kill anyone who threatened either of them. He was still all of these versions of himself, even if it seemed at times that some of them had ceased to exist.

If he was still all of these previous figures, therefore, it meant that at this moment he was also all of the future versions of himself that he would become: the retired widower, the pensioner struggling to live alone, the old man who sat all day in a wheelchair at the window of a nursing home, with his eyes closed as he vainly tried to recall once standing at some other window in a hotel in some foreign city whose name he had once known.

A bewildered, ancient man in a wheelchair, about to open his eyes and gaze out at the sweep of trees down an empty nursing home driveway, as if awaiting a visitor whose name he would not be able to remember. A demented man, no longer sure of his true identity or where he actually was, but who finally knew that he no longer needed to pretend to be acting out some role for anyone. A man who was certain only that he was alive and truly alone and he had no way of being certain about any other fact, no way of knowing what had actually occurred in his life and what had just been a transient illusion.

The End.